Finding My Blue Ribbon Pet

Written by: Rebecca Rose Taylor

Illustrations by: Fablana Garcia

Author photo by: Sheila Quinn

DEDICATION

This book is dedicated to all pet owners who give their pets a loving home, and to all of the pet rescues who care for animals in need until they can be adopted.

AUTHOR'S NOTE

Choosing a pet requires a lot of consideration, including the circumstances in which the pet will be living. The right pet for Cole, the little boy in the story, might not be the right pet for your family. And, likewise, a pet that Cole decides is boring etc. might be the right pet for you. This is a fictional story and not a guide on selecting the right pet for you.

My best day ever was when I finally got a pet. I was six. To start with I didn't have a pet and needed one. The pet show was one week away and I told my parents at supper that I needed the best pet ever because I wanted to win the blue ribbon.

"How about your Aunt Millie's cat?" said Dad.
"Everyone has a cat," I said.

"Maybe you could borrow the neighbour's dog," said Mom.
"Dogs are ordinary. I need something special to win the blue ribbon."

Then I saw a bug on the floor. I jumped up from the table to get a closer look, knocking over my chair. My baby sister started crying and Mom picked her up. The bug flew away before I could decide it if it could be a blue ribbon pet. It was too small anyways.

"Cole, you woke up Alice," said Mom giving me a look.
"I know! Alice could be the blue ribbon pet. I could put her in her Halloween costume. None of the kids would have anything like her."
"You cannot show your sister," said Dad.
"But Dad, I need the best pet ever."

"What kind of pets do your friends have?" asked Mom.
"Billy has a snake, but I think they're yucky."
"Snakes, ew" said Mom wiggling in her seat.

"Larry's got a mouse. It's cool and climbs his arm."
"No mice," said Mom.

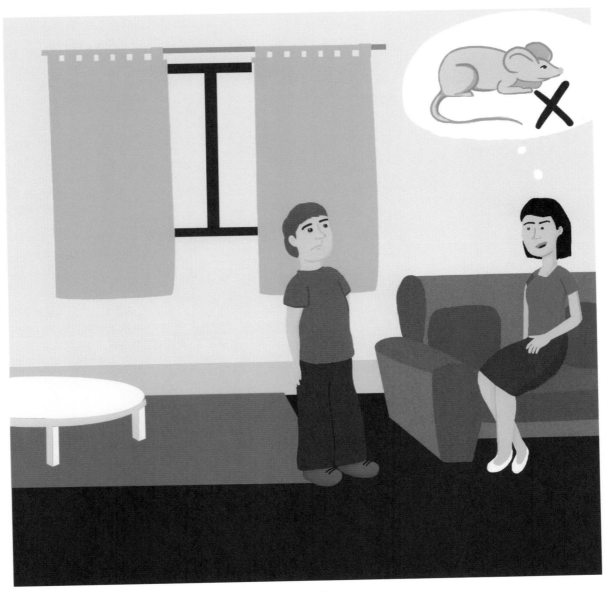

"How about we go visit the pet shop tomorrow?" said Dad.
"Can we?" I said clapping my hands.
"Yes," said Dad.

I looked at my animal books before I went to bed imagining the best pet ever. If we lived on a farm, then I would like to have a calf, but there's no room for one in our apartment. The bunnies and hamsters are cute but other kids in my class have one.

I was awake before Mom and Dad the next morning. I was ready to find my blue ribbon pet. When my Dad got up he said the pet store was still closed. I ran around the house pretending to be the winner of the blue ribbon.

When we walked into the pet store I saw the fish tanks. They looked like a bowl of rainbows. I knew they would be a boring pet.

Birds were in cages but I didn't want my blue ribbon pet flying away at the park.

I looked at the iguanas next; maybe they would be a fun pet. Some kinds could change colour and hide in their homes. One of these might have a chance at winning the blue ribbon.

I kept looking around because I had to make sure that I made the best choice not only for winning at the pet show, but also for having a pet that I loved after the show.

Then I saw the miniature pigs. They were cute, and made funny oinking noises when I petted them. I held one and it snorted and I laughed. I looked at the pictures around their pen. A lot of the pigs were wearing clothes. I thought they might be too girly for me. If I was on a farm, I knew I would like having pigs because they like playing in the mud like me.

I kept looking. Then I saw a pet store worker feeding a baby hedgehog. I knew that it would be my blue ribbon pet. We bought it and named him Needles. I still have the ribbon he got for being the most interesting pet at the show.

ABOUT THE AUTHOR

Rebecca Rose Taylor is an author from rural Quebec. She has loved creating stories even since before she could write them down herself. Rebecca lives on a farm and loves being able to work and play with her pets and the farm animals. They are one of her inspirations when it comes to writing. Spending time working in the barn also gives her time to brainstorm story ideas. Rebecca also enjoys other hobbies including reading, gardening and crocheting.

Thank you for reading
Finding My Blue Ribbon Pet.

29369340R00015

Printed in Great Britain
by Amazon